holiday

To Zachary & Noah–for Hanukkah,

to Akira & Noel–for Christmas,

and to Chloe, Ryan, Owen, Isaiah & Ginger–for both.

THIS IS A BORZOI BOOK PUBLISHED BY ALFRED A. KNOPF

Copyright © 2012 by Selina Alko

All rights reserved. Published in the United States by Alfred A. Knopf,
an imprint of Random House Children's Books, a division of Random House, Inc., New York.

Knopf, Borzoi Books, and the colophon are registered trademarks of Random House, Inc.

Visit us on the Web! randomhouse.com/kids

Educators and librarians, for a variety of teaching tools,
visit us at randomhouse.com/teachers

Library of Congress Cataloging-in-Publication Data
Daddy Christmas and Hanukkah Mama / Selina Alko. – 1st ed.
p. cm.
Summary: A child relates how the family celebrates both Christmas and Hanukkah,
enjoying the rich traditions of both religions.
ISBN 978-0-375-86093-5 (trade) – ISBN 978-0-375-96093-2 (lib. bdg)
[1. Christmas–Fiction. 2. Hanukkah–Fiction. 3. Family life–Fiction.] I. Title.
PZZA39843 Dad 2012
[E]–dc23
2011019230

The illustrations in this book were created using gouache, collage, and colored pencil on Arches watercolor paper.

MANUFACTURED IN MALAYSIA
September 2012
10 9 8 7 6 5 4 3 2 1

First Edition

DADDY
Christmas
& WITHDRAWN
Hanukkah
MAMA

by Selina Alko

Alfred A. Knopf • New York

I am a mix of two traditions.

From Daddy Christmas and Hanukkah Mama.

Our tree is crowned with one shiny star.

And we light eight candles for Hanukkah.

I help Mama hang stockings by the fireplace.

Daddy makes latkes to leave on the mantel with milk.

Grandma's recipe is Santa's favorite treat.

We decorate our home for the holidays.

Mama scatters golden gelt under the tree.

Daddy hooks candy canes on menorah branches.

I paint powder-blue angels and red-nosed reindeer.

They fly around our living room with the king and queen.

On ribbons, my decorations hang from the ceiling.

Songs for both Hanukkah and Christmas in hand,

we carol to the neighbors about Maccabees and the manger.

"Dreidel, Dreidel, Dreidel" and "Silent Night."

Mixing music to bright smiles.

I sing for both Daddy Christmas and Hanukkah Mama.

In the kitchen,

we prepare a festive meal,

just in time for the last night of Hanukkah.

Daddy stuffs the turkey with

cranberry kugel dressing.

Mama makes jelly donuts

and fruitcake for dessert.

I set the table for Savta, Saba, Granny, and aunts, uncles, and cousins.

Daddy Christmas and Hanukkah Mama will sit on each end, with me in the middle.

Watching snowflakes fall, we wait for family to arrive.

Everyone passes under the mistletoe, kissing me,

Hanukkah Mama, and Daddy Christmas hello.

Mountains of gifts are placed under the tree
for eight nights of Hanukkah,
plus Christmas Day.

How lucky am I?

When dinner's done, the family gathers in the living room.

Uncle Zachary recalls the miracle of the oil.

Aunt Faith tells about the animals in the manger,

waiting for the baby to be born.

Wide-eyed, we listen to these traditional tales,

which link us together today.

Christmas morning, I cannot wait to see
what is underneath the tree.
With mocha eggnog lattes,
Hanukkah Mama and Daddy Christmas
soon join me.

Daddy plays mellow holiday jazz.

Mama heats up leftover potato pancakes.

We take turns giving each other a final gift.

After New Year's Eve festivities,

we take down the tree, unstring the lights, and pack up the menorah.

I carefully place ornaments and dreidels inside a box.

Decorations go into storage for next year.

Daddy Christmas sweeps up pine needles,

and Hanukkah Mama tosses wrapping paper into the recycling bin.

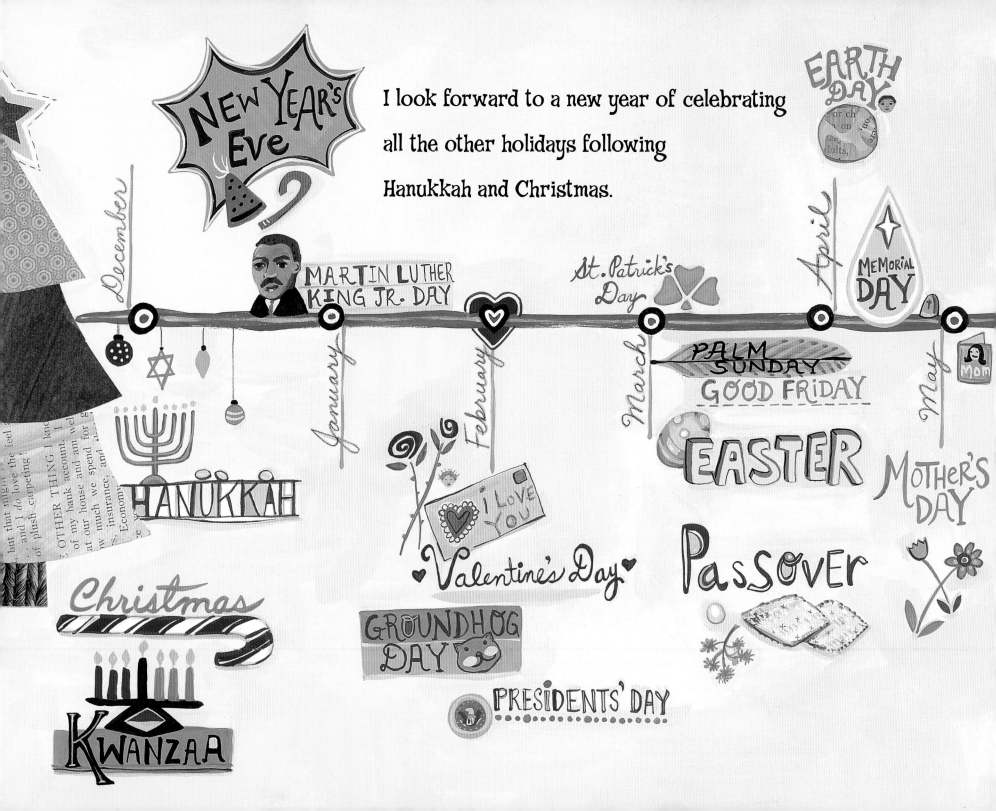

I look forward to a new year of celebrating all the other holidays following Hanukkah and Christmas.

With Daddy, Mama, and me.

CRANBERRY KUGEL DRESSING RECIPE

Cranberry Kugel

1/4 cup butter

4 eggs

3 cups cooked egg noodles

salt and pepper to taste

cinnamon and sugar to taste

1/3 cup dried cranberries

Melt the butter over medium heat on the stovetop. Beat the eggs and butter well and add to the cooked noodles. Pour into a baking dish. Season with the salt, pepper, cinnamon, and sugar. Add the dried cranberries. Bake at 350 degrees for one hour or until brown.

Dressing

1/2 cup chopped celery

1/2 cup chopped onion

1/4 cup butter

1/2 cup chopped mushrooms

2 tbsp. chopped parsley

cranberry kugel chopped in small pieces

salt and pepper to taste

In a large skillet, fry the celery and the onion in the butter until golden. Add the mushrooms and cook three minutes more. Add the parsley, chopped-up cranberry kugel, and salt and pepper, and stir.

Stuff your turkey with the dressing or eat the dressing plain.

Enjoy!